Rembrandt takes a Walk

Story by
Mark Strand

Illustrations by
Red Grooms

Tom's Uncle Morton was a tightwad. He had tons of money, but his car was old and his furniture was falling apart. He never bought new clothes. His shirts were frayed at the cuffs and collars, his socks had holes in the toes, and all his shoes were worn through. The only things he spent money on were paintings.

But he was so grouchy and his house was such a mess that nobody ever came to see the paintings.

"I think it's time for you to visit your Uncle Morton again," said Tom's mother. "He's getting lonely and you seem to be the only person who can cheer him up."

"I hate going there," said Tom. "His house is big and gloomy, and nothing works. And Uncle Morton never has any food around."

"But he's got those wonderful paintings," said Tom's mother, "and I hear he's added a new one!"

"I don't want to see paintings," said Tom. "I want to eat and watch TV."

"Well, just one more time, for your mom," said Tom's mother.

EVENING IN
THE MEADOWS

AELBERT CUYP
1620-1691

Clarkson N. Potter, Inc./Publishers

DISTRIBUTED BY CROWN PUBLISHERS, INC., NEW YORK

So Tom went to his rich Uncle Morton's
house to have dinner and spend the night.

Uncle Morton met him in a torn bathrobe,
which he wore over baggy pants and a crumpled
shirt. He looked like a bum.

"Hi, Uncle Morton," said Tom.

"Come in, my boy," said Uncle Morton.
He led Tom down a dark hallway into
the huge dining room, which was lit
by a single light bulb that
dangled from the ceiling.
"Dinner's ready,"
said Uncle Morton.

Tom saw two small dishes on the giant table.
On each dish was half a hamburger and a few
peas. It took only about a minute to eat dinner.

Then Uncle Morton invited Tom into his wood-paneled den to watch TV. It was an old black-and-white set that didn't work right. After a few minutes, Tom fell asleep in his chair and his Uncle Morton covered him with an old moth-eaten blanket.

The next morning Tom woke up early and went to the kitchen to get breakfast. But when he opened the refrigerator, it was empty. Uncle Morton had forgotten to buy any food. There wasn't any juice. There wasn't any milk. There was nothing in the cupboard either. No bread in the bread box. No cookies in the cookie jar.

Tom went into the dining room. He thought of waking Uncle Morton, but he didn't want to make him grouchy. He looked at one of the paintings on the wall. It was by Paul Cézanne, and it was filled with apples and oranges in dishes or spread out on a crumpled white tablecloth. Even though it was painted nearly a hundred years ago, it made Tom hungry. He stood on a chair to get a closer look. "Those apples look real good!" thought Tom. Then he touched the closest one. It moved. He touched another and it, too, moved.

Amazing! He shook the tablecloth and all the apples moved. "I wonder if I could eat those apples," thought Tom, and he reached into the painting and pulled one out, then put it on the table. "Maybe there's a better one in there." He reached in and pulled out another. Soon he had taken all the apples and oranges out. The painting looked very empty.

Next to Cézanne's there was a painting by the Spanish painter Francisco de Zurbarán. The oranges in it looked juicier even though they were painted over *three* hundred years ago.

Tom got on a chair to see if he could reach into the painting and take out its oranges. Sure enough, he could. He emptied the pretty basket of its oranges and put them on the table with Cézanne's apples and oranges. And he took the lemons from the little silver dish as well.

The table was covered with fruit, and both paintings were empty. Tom was suddenly worried. Suppose Uncle Morton woke up and came downstairs! He'd better put everything back. He started, but he couldn't quite remember where things went. He put some Zurbarán lemons in the Cézanne and some Cézanne apples in the Zurbarán. And neither painting looked right. Tom was *very* worried.

He tried several times to rearrange the fruit, but the paintings looked even worse. Eating the apples didn't make it any easier.

No sooner had he sat down than he heard . . .

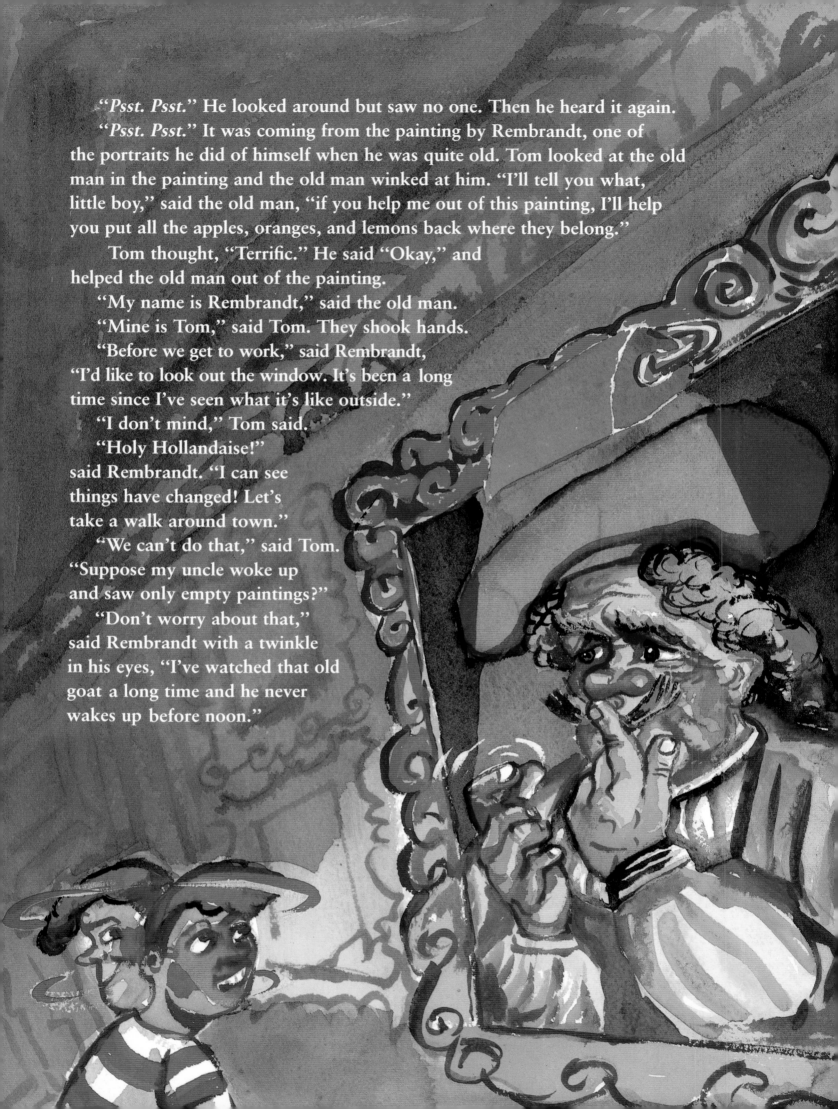

"*Psst. Psst.*" He looked around but saw no one. Then he heard it again.

"*Psst. Psst.*" It was coming from the painting by Rembrandt, one of the portraits he did of himself when he was quite old. Tom looked at the old man in the painting and the old man winked at him. "I'll tell you what, little boy," said the old man, "if you help me out of this painting, I'll help you put all the apples, oranges, and lemons back where they belong."

Tom thought, "Terrific." He said "Okay," and helped the old man out of the painting.

"My name is Rembrandt," said the old man.

"Mine is Tom," said Tom. They shook hands.

"Before we get to work," said Rembrandt, "I'd like to look out the window. It's been a long time since I've seen what it's like outside."

"I don't mind," Tom said.

"Holy Hollandaise!" said Rembrandt. "I can see things have changed! Let's take a walk around town."

"We can't do that," said Tom. "Suppose my uncle woke up and saw only empty paintings?"

"Don't worry about that," said Rembrandt with a twinkle in his eyes, "I've watched that old goat a long time and he never wakes up before noon."

"But you're not dressed right," said Tom. "You've got to take off that turban and funny coat. My uncle has a suit in the closet upstairs that might fit you."

Tom and Rembrandt tiptoed upstairs where Rembrandt put on the suit. It was moth-eaten and creased and a little tight, but it looked a lot better than what Rembrandt had been wearing. "That looks good," said Tom, "but I think you should put on a necktie, too. You'll look a little dressier, if you know what I mean." Tom was beginning to sound like his mother.

Rembrandt got on his knees, and Tom, who had just learned how to tie a necktie, tied Rembrandt's for him. "Nobody wore these things back in my day," said Rembrandt, admiring himself in the mirror.

When they left the house Rembrandt took a deep breath. "It feels good to breathe fresh air again," he said.

"Let's walk toward the center of town," said Tom. The sky was blue, dotted with pure white clouds. Birds sang in the leafy trees. Rembrandt began whistling a tune that Tom didn't recognize. "Say," said Rembrandt, "you know what I'd like to do? I'd like to draw." He reached into his shirt and pulled out some sheets of paper. "I never go anywhere without something to draw on," he said. "All I need now is something to draw with."

"Look in the jacket pocket," said Tom. Sure enough, Rembrandt found lots of stubby pencils.

Rembrandt leaned over the hood of a car and started to draw a house and trees. "Great Gouda!" he yelled, "Three hundred years make a tremendous difference. I'm rusty. I've lost my touch."

Tom looked at the drawing. "It looks pretty good to me," he said.

"Nonsense," said Rembrandt. "You should've seen me in my prime. I don't like to brag, but I was fabulous. Come with me," said Rembrandt as he pulled Tom after him. Finally, they stopped in front of the fire station.

"Now that's what I call a carriage," said Rembrandt.

"That's no carriage," said Tom, "that's a fire engine."

"You don't say," said Rembrandt, and he started to draw. Tom stood under a tree, waiting for him to finish.

"If only I had some paint and a canvas," said Rembrandt.

"We have to go now," said Tom.

"Wait," said Rembrandt.

"I just want to finish up the wheels."

Rembrandt stood up and looked around. A few houses down, a woman was watering her flowers. "Look at that beautiful woman over there," said Rembrandt. "What flesh." And he dashed over with his pencils and paper. But when the woman saw a man on her lawn, staring wild-eyed at her, she ran into her house.

Rembrandt was knocking on her front door when Tom shouted, "No, no, you can't do that. We've got to get back."

"But I don't want to get back," said Rembrandt. "I want to keep drawing. I may never get another chance."

"Yes, you will," said Tom, thinking fast. "If you come back to my uncle's house now and go back into the painting, I'll come over as soon as I can and take you out for another walk."

"Will you bring me some pens and ink and good drawing paper?" asked Rembrandt.

"I promise," said Tom.

"Will you bring some paint and canvas?" asked Rembrandt.

"I'll try," said Tom.

"Okay, then let's go," said Rembrandt with a big smile.

On the way back to the house, Rembrandt said nothing. Tom thought of pointing out TV aerials, telephone poles, electric lights, lawn mowers, and lots of other things, but he knew that Rembrandt would want to stop and draw them—and there wasn't time.

When they got back
the house was quiet.
Uncle Morton was not
up yet. There was still time
to get the paintings the way
they belonged. But before
he got to work, Rembrandt took
off Uncle Morton's suit.

"I like this tie. I think I'll keep
it on a while," he said.

"Okay," said Tom. "But don't
forget to take it off when you're done."

Tom carried his uncle's suit
upstairs where he hung it back up in the
closet. When Tom came down, Rembrandt was
working on the Cézanne but rearranging it
to suit himself. "I think I like it this way," said
Rembrandt, stepping back for a good look.
Suddenly Tom heard Uncle Morton cough and
the door to his bedroom open. "We *have* to put it
back the way Cézanne had it and we've got to *hurry*,"
he told Rembrandt. "My uncle is coming!"

"There!" said Rembrandt, doing some quick
switching, "For what it's worth."

"Are you downstairs, Tom?" called Uncle Morton. "Is that you I hear?"

"It's me, Uncle Morton," Tom called back.

Rembrandt was already stepping from the chair back into his painting. He was halfway in when he turned around to wave good-bye to Tom.

Tom waved back but saw that Rembrandt had forgotten to take off Uncle Morton's tie.

"Ah, admiring my Rembrandt," said Uncle Morton. "Beautiful isn't it? Every time I look at it, I discover something new in it," said Uncle Morton.

Tom's face turned bright red. He thought for sure his uncle would see the tie.

"No need to be embarrassed, my boy," said Uncle Morton. "That painting's a masterpiece."

"Maybe we should go out and have breakfast," Tom said.

"Good idea," said Uncle Morton. "Let's go to your house. I bet your mom will make us something real good."

"Good idea," said Tom. And off they went to Tom's house where Tom's mother made them a delicious breakfast of tall glasses of juice, big bowls of cereal, sausages, and stacks of french toast smothered in butter and maple syrup.

Published by Clarkson N. Potter, Inc., 225 Park Avenue South, New York, New York 10003 and represented in Canada by the Canadian MANDA Group

CLARKSON N. POTTER, POTTER, and colophon are trademarks of Clarkson N. Potter, Inc.
Manufactured in Japan

Library of Congress Cataloging-in-Publication Data
Strand, Mark
Rembrandt takes a walk.
Summary: On a visit to his rich eccentric uncle, Tom discovers his painting have some unusual qualities, such as when Rembrandt leaves his self-portrait and takes a walk with Tom.
[1. Fantasy. 2. Painting—Fiction. 3. Rembrandt Harmenszoon van Rijn, 1606-1699—Fiction]
I. Grooms, Red, ill.   II. Title.
PZ7.S8967Re 1986   [Fic]   86-3260
ISBN 0-517-56293-6
10 9 8 7 6 5 4 3 2 1
First Edition